THUNDER ROSE

JERDINE NOLEN

Illustrated by

KADIR NELSON

VOYAGER BOOKS
HARCOURT, INC.

Orlando   Austin   New York   San Diego   Toronto   London

For information about permission to reproduce selections from this book,
please write Permissions, Houghton Mifflin Harcourt Publishing Company
215 Park Avenue South, NY, NY 10003.

www.hmhco.com

First Voyager Books edition 2007

Voyager Books is a trademark of Harcourt, Inc.,
registered in the United States of America and/or other jurisdictions.

The Library of Congress has cataloged the hardcover edition as follows:
Nolen, Jerdine.
Thunder Rose/Jerdine Nolen; illustrated by Kadir Nelson.
p. cm.
Summary: Unusual from the day she is born, Thunder Rose performs all sorts of amazing feats,
including building metal structures, taming a stampeding herd of steers,
capturing a gang of rustlers, and turning aside a tornado.
[1. Tall tales.] I. Nelson, Kadir, ill. II. Title.
PZ7.N723Th 2003
[E]—dc21 2002012287
ISBN 978-0-15-216472-0
ISBN 978-0-15-206006-0 pb

LEO 10 9 8 7
4500587123

The art was prepared with oil, watercolor, and pencil.
The display lettering was created by Jane Dill.
The text type was set in Meridien Medium.
Color separations by Bright Arts Ltd., Hong Kong
Manufactured by LEO,China
Production supervision by Christine Witnik
Designed by Judythe Sieck

AUTHOR'S NOTE

For as long as I can remember, I have wanted to contribute to the long tradition of American folklore by writing a tall tale set in the Old West. Some who settled that land were Africans who had been treated as slaves in the South. It is a little-known part of American history, but as the Civil War came to an end, these bold, brave, and adventurous spirits heroically took the opportunity to set themselves down in those wide-open spaces to live free.

Though many black folktales were created out of sorrow, an imaginative healing power resonates within them. I knew I wanted to construct a tale out of love and joy, one told from the perspective of that "fortunate feeling" that dwells deep within each of us. A child of this particular type of fortune might be Thunder Rose, cowgirl heroine of the West.

Rose was the first child born free and easy to Jackson and Millicent MacGruder. I recall most vividly the night she came into this world. Hailing rain, flashing lightning, and booming thunder pounded the door, inviting themselves in for the blessed event.

Taking in her first breath of life, the infant did not cry out. Rather, she sat up and looked around. She took hold of that lightning, rolled it into a ball, and set it above her shoulder, while the thunder echoed out over the other. They say this just accentuated the fact that the child had the power of thunder and lightning coursing through her veins.

"She's going to grow up to be good and strong, all right," Doc Hollerday said.

The child turned to the good doctor with a thoughtful glance and replied, "I reckon I will want to do more than that. Thank you very kindly!"

Shifting her gaze to the two loving lights shining on her, which were her ma and pa, she remarked, "Much obliged to you both for this chance to make my way in the world!" Then she announced to no one in particular, "I am right partial to the name Rose."

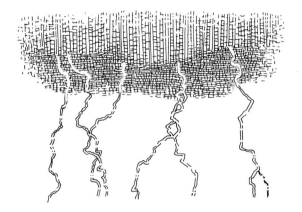

So much in love with this gift of their lives, her ma and pa hovered over her in watchful splendor. Overcome with that love, they lifted their voices in song, an old song and a melody so sweet and true—a lullaby passed down from the ages, echoing since the beginning of time.

"There is a music ringing so sweetly in my ears," the newborn exclaimed. "It's giving me a fortunate feeling rumbling deep in the pit of me. I'll register it here at the bull's-eye set in the center of my heart, and see what I can do with it one day!"

Rose snored up plenty that first night breathing on her own, rattling the rafters on the roof right along with the booming thunder. There was nothing quiet about her slumber. She seemed determined to be just as forceful as that storm. With the thunder and lightning keeping watch over her the rest of the night, her ma and pa just took to calling her Thunder Rose.

The next morning, when the sun was high yellow in that billowy blue sky, Rose woke up hungry as a bear in spring, but not the least bit ornery. Minding her manners, she politely thanked her ma for the milk, but it was not enough to quench her hungry thirst. Rose preferred, instead, to drink her milk straight from the cow.

Her ma was right grateful to have such a resourceful child. No other newborn had the utter strength to lift a whole cow clear over her head and almost drink it dry. In a moment's time, Rose did, and quite daintily so. She was as pretty as a picture, had the sweetest disposition, but don't let yourself be misled, that child was full of lightning *and* thunder.

Out on that paper-bag brown, dusty dry, wide-open space, Rose often was found humming a sweet little tune as she did her chores. And true to her word, Rose did *more* than grow good and strong.

The two-year-old became quite curious about the pile of scrap iron lying next to the barn. Rose took a good-sized piece, stretched it here, bent and twisted it there. She constructed a thunderbolt as black as pitch to punctuate her name. She called it Cole. Wherever she went, Cole was always by her side. Noticing how skilled Rose was with the metal, her pa made sure there was an extra supply of it always around.

At the age of five, Rose did a commendable job of staking the fence without a bit of help. During her eighth and ninth years, Rose assembled some iron beams together with the wood blocks she used to play with and constructed a building tall enough to scrape the sky, always humming as she worked.

By the time she turned twelve, Rose had perfected her metal-bending practices. She formed delicately shaped alphabet letters to help the young ones learn to read. For his birthday, Rose presented her pa with a branding iron, a circle with a big *M-A-C* for MacGruder in the middle, just in time, too, because a herd of quick-tempered longhorn steer was stampeding its way up from the Rio Grande. They were plowing a path straight toward her front door.

Rose performed an eye-catching wonder, the likes
of which was something to see. Running lightning-fast
toward the herd, using Cole for support, Rose vaulted into
the air and landed on the back of the biggest lead steer
like he was a merry-go-round pony. Grabbing a horn in
each hand, Rose twisted that varmint to a complete halt.
It was just enough to restrain that top bull and the rest of
the herd.

But I believe what touched that critter's heart was when Rose began humming her little tune. That cantankerous ton of beef was restless no more. He became as playful as a kitten and even tried to purr. Rose named him Tater on account of that was his favorite vegetable. Hearing Rose's lullaby put that considerable creature to sleep was the sweetest thing I had witnessed in a long, long time.

After the dust had settled, Ma and Pa counted twenty-seven hundred head of cattle, after they added in the five hundred they already had. Using the scrap iron, Rose had to add a new section to the bull pen to hold them all.

"What did you do to the wire, Rose?" Ma asked, surprised and pleased at her daughter's latest creation.

"Oh, that," she said. "While I was staking the fence, Pa asked me to keep little Barbara Jay company. That little twisty pattern seemed to make the baby laugh. So I like to think of it as Barbara's Wire."

"That was right clever of you to be so entertaining to the little one like that!" her ma said. Rose just blushed. Over the years, that twisty wire caught on, and folks just called it barbed wire.

Rose and her pa spent the whole next day sorting the animals that had not been branded. "One day soon, before the cold weather gets in," she told her pa, "I'll have to get this herd up the Chisholm Trail and to market in Abilene. I suspect Tater is the right kind of horse for the long drive northward."

On Rose's first trip to Abilene, while right outside of Caldwell, that irascible, full-of-outrage-and-ire outlaw Jesse Baines and his gang of desperadoes tried to rustle that herd away from Rose.

Using the spare metal rods she always carried with her, Rose lassoed those hot-tempered hooligans up good and tight. She dropped them all off to jail, tied up in a nice neat iron bow. "It wasn't any trouble at all," she told Sheriff Weaver. "Somebody had to put a stop to their thieving ways."

But that wasn't the only thieving going on. The mighty sun was draining the moisture out of every living thing it touched. Even the rocks were crying out. Those clouds stood by and watched it all happen. They weren't even trying to be helpful.

Why, the air had turned so dry and sour, time seemed to all but stand still. And there was not a drop of water in sight. Steer will not move without water. And that was making those bulls mad, real mad. And when a bull gets angry, it's like a disease that's catching, making the rest of the herd mad, too. Tater was looking parched and mighty thirsty.

"I've got to do something about this!" Rose declared.

Stretching out several iron rods lasso-fashion, then launching Cole high in the air, Rose hoped she could get the heavens to yield forth. She caught hold of a mass of clouds and squeezed them hard, real hard, all the while humming her song. Gentle rain began to fall. But anyone looking could see there was not enough moisture to refresh two ants, let alone a herd of wild cows.

Suddenly a rotating column of air came whirling and swirling around, picking up everything in its path. It sneaked up on Rose. "Whoa, there, now just hold on a minute," Rose called out to the storm. Tater was helpless to do anything about that sort of wind. Those meddlesome clouds caused it. They didn't take kindly to someone telling them what to do. And they were set on creating a riotous rampage all on their own.

Oh, this riled Rose so much, she became the only two-legged tempest to walk the western plains. "You don't know who you're fooling with," Rose called out to the storm. Her eyes flashed lightning. She bit down and gnashed thunder from her teeth. I don't know why anyone would want to mess with a pretty young woman who had the power of thunder and lightning coursing through her veins. But, pity for them, the clouds did!

Rose reached for her iron rod. But there was only one piece left. She did not know which way to turn. She knew Cole alone was not enough to do the job right. Unarmed against her own growing thirst and the might of the elements, Rose felt weighted down. Then that churning column split, and now there were two. They were coming at her from opposite directions. Rose had some fast thinking to do. Never being one to bow down under pressure, she considered her options, for she was not sure how this would all come out in the end.

"Is this the fork in the road with which I have my final supper? Will this be my first and my last ride of the roundup?" she queried herself in the depths of her heart. Her contemplations brought her little relief as she witnessed the merciless, the cataclysmic efforts of a windstorm bent on her disaster. Then the winds joined hands and cranked and churned a path heading straight toward her! Calmly Rose spoke out loud to the storm as she stood alone to face the wrack and ruin, the multiplying devastation. "I *could* ride at least *one* of you out to the end of time! But I've got this fortunate feeling rumbling deep in the pit of me, and I see what I am to do with it this day!" Rose said, smiling.

The winds belted at a rumbling pitch. Rose squarely faced that storm. "Come and join me, winds!" She opened her arms wide as if to embrace the torrent. She opened her mouth as if she were planning to take a good long drink. But from deep inside her, she heard a melody so real and sweet and true. And when she lifted her heart, she unleashed *her* song of thunder. It was a sight to see: Rose making thunder and lightning rise and fall to the ground at her command, at the sound of *her song*. Oh, how her voice rang out so clear and real and true. It rang from the mountaintops. It filled up the valleys. It flowed like a healing river in the breathing air around her.

Those tornadoes, calmed by her song, stopped their churning masses and raged no more. And, gentle as a baby's bath, a soft, drenching-and-soaking rain fell.

And Rose realized that by reaching into her own heart to
bring forth the music that was there, she had even touched
the hearts of the clouds.

The stories of Rose's amazing abilities spread
like wildfire, far and wide. And as sure as thunder
follows lightning, and sun follows rain, whenever
you see a spark of light flash across a heavy steel

gray sky, listen to the sound of the thunder and think of Thunder Rose and *her* song. That mighty, mighty song pressing on the bull's-eye that was set at the center of her heart.